THE
SANDCASTLE
THAT LOLA BUILT

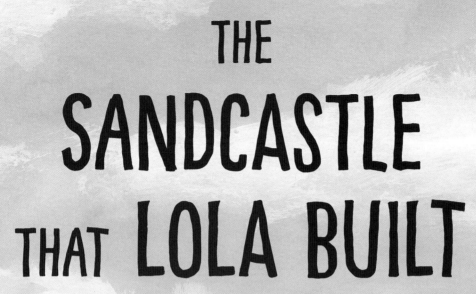

by Megan Maynor

illustrated by Kate Berube

Alfred A. Knopf
New York

THIS IS A BORZOI BOOK PUBLISHED BY ALFRED A. KNOPF

Text copyright © 2018 by Megan Maynor
Jacket art and interior illustrations copyright © 2018 by Kate Berube

Visit us on the Web! rhcbooks.com

Educators and librarians, for a variety of teaching tools,
visit us at RHTeachersLibrarians.com

Library of Congress Cataloging-in-Publication Data
Names: Maynor, Megan, author. | Berube, Kate, illustrator.
Title: The sandcastle that Lola built / by Megan Maynor ; illustrated by Kate Berube.
Description: First edition. | New York : Alfred A. Knopf, [2018] | Summary: As Lola builds a sandcastle, she is joined by Frisbee Dude, Little Guy,
and Minnesota Girl in a story reminiscent of "The House that Jack Built." | Identifiers: LCCN 2016035888 (print) | LCCN 2017012679 (ebook) |
ISBN 978-1-5247-1615-8 (trade) | ISBN 978-1-5247-1616-5 (lib. bdg.) | ISBN 978-1-5247-1617-2 (ebook)
Subjects: | CYAC: Sandcastles—Fiction. | Cooperativeness—Fiction.
Classification: LCC PZ7.1.M388 (ebook) | LCC PZ7.1.M388 San 2018 (print) | DDC [E]—dc23

The text of this book is set in 17.5-point Jacoby ICG Light.
The illustrations in this book were created using mixed media and collage
on cold press watercolor paper.

MANUFACTURED IN CHINA
May 2018
10 9 8 7 6 5 4
First Edition

For my parents, Norb and Pat Gernes,
who took me many places, including the beach
—M.M.

For my mom, for instilling in me the belief that I could become an artist
(and also, for all those wonderful days spent at the beach!)
—K.B.

This is the sandcastle that Lola built.

This is the
tall,
tall
tower

Of the sandcastle
that Lola built.

This is the
sea glass

That signals mermaids
From the tall, tall tower
Of the sandcastle that Lola built.

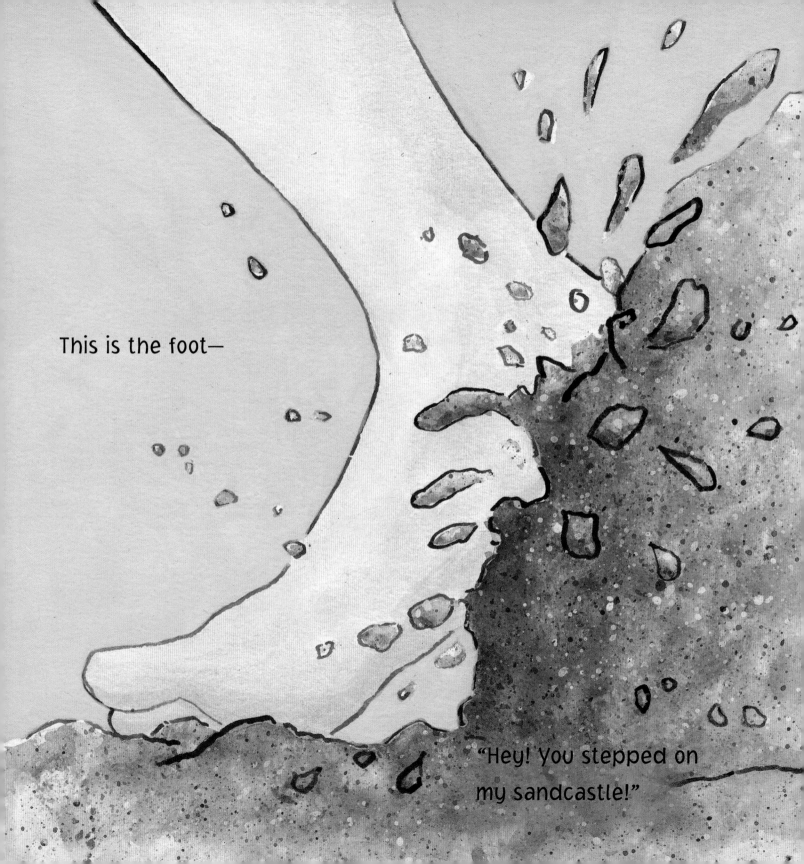

"Oh," said the dude with a Frisbee. "Oops."
"You can use this bucket to fix it," said Lola.
"Okay . . ."

"What should we add next?" asked Lola.
"We?"

This is the wall
That protects the castle

That holds the sea glass
That signals mermaids

From the
    tall,
        tall
            tower

Of the sandcastle that Lola and Frisbee Dude built.

"Dig!" said the little guy.

"You can dig here instead, and help with our sandcastle."

"Dig?" asked the little guy. "More?"

"Yes," said Lola. "More!"

This is the bulldozer
That dug the moat
That surrounds the wall
That protects the castle

That holds the sea glass
That signals mermaids
From the
   tall,
      tall
         tower

Of the sandcastle that Lola and
Frisbee Dude and Little Guy built.

These are the shells—

SPLASH!

"Oh no!" said Lola.

"Here, you can have some of mine," said the girl.

"You found all these?" asked Lola.

The girl nodded. "I'm bringing them home to Minnesota, so I can remember the ocean."

"Do you want to add shells to our sandcastle?"

"You bet!"

These are the shells

That lead to the moat

That surrounds the wall

That protects the castle

That holds the sea glass
That signals mermaids
From the
tall,
tall tower

Of the sandcastle that Lola and Frisbee Dude and
Little Guy and Minnesota Girl built.

This is the—

"No way!" said Frisbee Dude.

"Uh-oh!" said Little Guy.

"That's not good," said Minnesota Girl.

Lola sniffed. "The mermaids didn't even get to move in yet."
She packed up her pails.

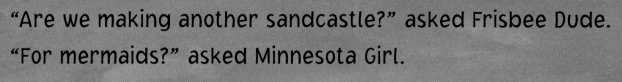

"Are we making another sandcastle?" asked Frisbee Dude.
"For mermaids?" asked Minnesota Girl.
"Again?" asked Little Guy.

"We?" asked Lola.

"I'll find more shells!"

"I could . . . build a tall, tall tower?" said Lola.

"Hooray!"